BROKEN TO DUST

IESHA SHAW

ISBN: 978-1-956653-09-0 (Paperback)

ISBN: 978-1-956653-10-6 (Hardcover)

For Janet, with love.

CONTENTS

1

FRIENDS OR LOVERS

"Chief, I have a case file the social worker from Children's Special Services just brought over." The Detective known as Red hit his palm with the bottom of the manilla file folder as he closed the front door. Meanwhile, Janet Shaw's youngest son Willie Jr. was being shuffled down the drive to The State of Alabama Child Services van by Sabrina Bobay, the state social worker.

"Well, is there anything in there that can help us with this case?" The Chief asked.

"Well, ya' know Chief -"

"Mr. Red, Mr. Red. I don't want to go with this lady. Can you take me to the hospital to visit my mama?" Willie Jr. burst through the front door.

Red and the Chief exchanged glances. Red got down on Willie Jr.'s level. "Now Willie Jr., you know we talked about this when you first came home from school. The nice social worker from Birmingham-"

Red paused to read the file folder he had propped against his knee for her name. "Uh Ms. Bo- Bobay. She's gonna take you and yo' brother with her, on up to Birmingham for a nice stay in a motel. It's gonna be just like a vacation for you."

"But I don't know her," Willie jr. whined. "And you don't know her either. You just had to look her name up in that file."

The Chief had come over to stand next to Red for two reasons, for support and to block Willie Jr.'s view of the team of crime scene workers in his apartment and the criminal they held in the back.

"He's got ya' with that one, Red," the Chief said while grabbing his belt loops.

"Chief and Mr. Red, remember last year when you came and talked to us in the gym at school? You said to never go with strangers."

"Yes, I remember that Willie Jr. But I also told you - you can trust the police and their friends, like firemen, ambulance workers, and doctors and nurses. And you can add social workers to that list Willie Jr. I will vouch for Ms. Bobay. She's a friend of the police."

The youngest son of Janet Shaw, Willie Jr. had arrived from school on the bus earlier and the Chief had headed him off from entering the house.

"Okay, I'll go with her, but when can I see my mama? And where are my brothers?"

"Now don't you worry about Javari and Adreion, they're just fine. We'll have you all together by morning. As a matter of fact, your brother Adreion was just here before you made it home from school today. We sent him over to the police station to get some snacks. Me and the Chief are headed over there directly to speak to him about how yo mama ended up needing the ambulance and then he'll be coming to join you on your stay with Ms. Bobay."

"Well, okay, but that's not fair. I want some snacks like Adreion."

Ms. Bobay was now standing in the doorway, clutching a briefcase in front of her with both hands.

"I'll tell you what," Chief said as he pulled out a twenty-dollar bill. "If you go with this gracious lady (who may I remind you is a friend to the police), she'll stop you on down to the store over yonder near Highway 11 and grab you plenty of snacks. Is that alright?" Chief handed the twenty-dollar bill to Ms. Bobay.

"Well, I guess that's alright. But what about Mama?"

"Little Willie Jr. I can say with confidence that going with this lady is something your Mama would want for you. You'll just have to trust me on that."

"Well, when can I see my mama and talk to her myself?"

"Ms. Bobay is gonna talk to you all about that once you and your brothers are all settled in at the motel this evening. And I'll be by to check on you in the morning, Okay?"

"Okay, I guess."

"Good. Now that that's settled, here Ms. Bobay, you take this and get my friend Willie Jr. all his favorite snacks." He said this as he once again tried to hand Ms. Bobay the $20 bill.

"Before dinner, Chief?"

"My mama says boiled peanuts are a healthy snack even before dinner," Willie Jr. pleaded.

"Well, there you go. Take my friend Willie Jr. to that little mom and pop store on Highway 11 and get him some boiled peanuts."

"Chief, I can't take your money. But don't worry, we'll stop by and grab some boiled peanuts Willie Jr.," Sabrina Bobay reached for Willie Jr.'s hand.

JANET SHAW, a mother of three, had her first son Javari while in high school. She later attended college, where she undertook a course on business management while working part-time at a fast-food restaurant. She bore her second son, Adreion, after dropping out of college about a year later.

Being a single mother, Janet had left the children alone at a tender age, while she took on a full-time job to manage her finances. Burger King hired her as a manager. She was effectively involved in recruiting employees, overseeing operations, handling customer complaints, generating financial reports, and managing inventory. As a manager, you can imagine how overloaded with work she was. Having a life outside of taking care of her children was something she knew could no longer be a reality. But she could dream, and when she dreamed, it was of one person.

Willie Bell was a young, tall, handsome man with a neat haircut. He was attractive with shiny brown eyes, which matched perfectly with his complexion. Willie worked at Burger King as a chef and team leader. He had caught Janet's eye ever since they'd begun working together. Willie would assist her with financial reports and inventory since he had experience and was familiar with the management at the restaurant; this drew them to work together frequently.

As time went on, the two colleagues got along well. They would spend most of their free time and days together talking at work while managing the restaurant as Willie managed the kitchen. The more they talked and shared work experiences, home life and Janet's children, the closer they became as friends. It felt good for both of them to have an authentic human connection.

Within a few months, they were full-fledged friends and not the superficial kind. They were so close Janet introduced Willie to her children. Willie and Janet had all the ingredients to be best friends or possibly more, if they could admit it to themselves. They both had just gotten out of relationships and neither of them thought realistically they were in a place to want more or give more than a friendship.

The two friends and work colleagues eventually visited each other at home. Willie enjoyed his stay at Janet's place and the company of the kids on weekends and after work. The kids enjoyed his company too and always looked forward to his next visit when they would watch movies or television shows together. Willie easily blended in with the family. He was playful, and a clown; the kids enjoyed that all the more. The house was full of laughter and giggles from every corner whenever he was around.

Willie would occasionally surprise Janet with restaurant reservations during holidays and on weekends. This always included Janet's children. They would spend weekends in separate bedrooms in the mountains of Tennessee frolicking in the snow with the children, riding motorbikes together, and even camping. As hard workers on their 9-5, they enjoyed these leisurely moments.

Watching her children happier than she had ever seen them before, Janet developed feelings for Willie. He also had a secret crush on her. It seems the only obstacle holding their full happiness back was the knowledge of the other's heart, as neither of them realized the way the other felt. From the outside and from each of their own perspectives, their relationship seemed innocent enough.

Eventually, Janet and Willie were inseparable. At work, every chance they could get, they shared conversation, daily. With a cloak of warmth, Janet's heart skipped a beat at the thought of Willie whenever she pulled up at work. "Keep it together, Janet," she reprimanded herself in the car before work. "Don't go in there smiling too big and showing your whole hand - your whole heart, really." She would have to fight against her facial expressions, which threatened to give away her heart in the presence of Willie.

Yes, it became clear to Janet that her closeness with Willie had grown into a snowball of emotions she had to fight hard to control. So much passion loomed inside of her she thought she would burst. Her heart fought against her brain and threatened to do all the driving of her emotions. Almost unconsciously, she gave in to her compulsion to be around him all the time. At work, she would lose concentration and focus on anything she was supposed to be working on at the sight of him. She did not want to miss a moment of his essence or the opportunity for another day to spend time with him.

One day, when Janet was in a love daze waiting for Willie to arrive at work, he snuck up on her. "Hi, you look beautiful," he said as he offered her his hands and woke her from her trance.

"Thank you," she replied as she stretched her hands out to Willie. He stretched out his hands in response. They were ever so careful not to let their bodies touch or wrap their arms around each other. So, from three feet away Willie would stretch out his arms, and from that distance Janet would meet his hands, keeping her body three feet away, then they would clasp hands, and each gave a gentle squeeze. This was their new daily custom. Sometimes they'd lock eyes, gaze at one another and then flicker their stare away before it became awkward or taken as flirting.

"What do you think about that, Janet?"

Shoot! What did he ask me? I think you have so much

wisdom, Willie, that whatever you choose will be fine, she replied, hoping she had miraculously seemed to stay on whatever subject he was on.

Janet mostly listened to Willie talk about his life with little feedback other than a nod, a smile and a hmm umm in agreement. She often got lost in her own thoughts, staring at his parted lips as he spoke. Everything Willie Bell said was interesting to her no matter what it was because it caused all the features on his face to do a dance for her to watch. An eyebrow would furrow when there was something that frustrated him. A dimple would appear in the nano-second it took the corners of his lips to round and produce a smile. There was a special wrinkle that appeared on his forehead every time Willie tilted his head back to laugh. Janet longed to glide her fingers across that wrinkle someday. Then, just as quickly as she would hope for it, Janet would scold herself for her dreams, which she knew weren't realistic.

Janet listened intently to Willie more with her heart than with her ears. Ironic enough as interesting as she found him, she could have never recited what he said back if he would have asked, because usually the whole time he was talking, while she was watching his mouth work, she was thinking about them, together, off somewhere without the kids, on a date by candlelight. She loved taking him all in, watching his full lips.

"You and Willie getting together?" One of her coworkers, Larita, had asked.

"No girl, we're just friends. Besides, I don't think Willie is looking for a woman right now and I've got my plate full taking care of my kids."

"Hum hum," Larita smirked. "Keep on telling yourself that. I think that man's sweet on you and if you feel the same way, you'd better say something before it's too late. A man like him ain't gonna stay single for long."

While Willie was working on the grill, Janet gave his entire body a once over with her eyes. *Wow, Larita's right, this man is handsome.* She reflected on the happy moments she and Willie had been having together, and how the kids loved him. In that moment, Janet fantasized about what it would be like to be a real family. She even secretly wished for it. Still, because of her insecurities, which included being heavy set and a woman with a ready-made family as a single mother with two kids, Janet just wouldn't allow herself to go there. *I'm not setting myself up for that kind of disappointment. Besides, I'm not pretty enough for Willie, anyway. I'm sure he's looking for a girly girl who is free of attachments, not someone like me.*

Now, of course, Willie did not know Janet was battling with these doubts and self-esteem issues. What he did know was that from his perspective, Janet was daily playing a game of cat and mouse with him. *I'm not going to keep playing these games with this woman,* he thought to himself. Still in his quiet time at home, Willie couldn't get Janet off his mind. Hadn't he seen those beautiful eyes gleam every time he walked in her door? Or was he just imagining it?

Without warning, the last time he had the privilege of staring into those beautiful eyes at work, he found himself in the line of fire of Janet's fury. Willie reflected on his last encounter at work with Janet and how her eyebrows had knitted together and the gleam in her eyes seemed to turn dark. *What is it that could have brought that on?* He asked himself.

Willie kept turning that day's events repeatedly in his head. *Let's see, I came into work that day. Janet and I were playful with each other, just like we always are. She went on a break. That's when my niece came up there to get the money I'd promised to contribute to her prom dress. I remember now. When Janet walked in, I said,* "Let me introduce you to my-" *and I couldn't get the words out because Janet turned into a drill sergeant manager on me, out of nowhere.*

"Willie, if you have time to be up here in the front fraternizing with the guests, then you have time to clean out the freezer in the back."

"Do you have some business here, young lady?"

"No ma'am, I was just leaving." Willie's niece nervously replied.

Willie had quickly gone to the back and rotated and restocked the freezer inventory. By the time he was done, another worker had brought a list Janet had made up for him to work on that essentially kept him away from her most of the day. After a few hours of this, Janet locked herself in her office "doing paperwork."

MOST OF THE employees were in disbelief. Janet was always friendly and outgoing. She made working at Burger King fun. Today she was unapproachable, and if she did speak with anyone, it was to bark orders at them. When payroll was finished and there was no work left that Janet could do that would justify her staying locked in the manager's office any longer, she declared, "I'm leaving." And clocked out of work.

"Janet, wait," Willie pleaded.

Janet looked back and nearly fell trying to make it to the door before Willie could catch up with her. She clumsily unlocked her door and skidded out of the parking lot for home, talking to herself all the way there.

"I don't know who Willie thinks he is having that girl

come up here. I guess he likes them young and pretty, just like I figured. Well, I don't need no man. I'm just going to focus on my two children. I've had enough heartache in my life, and I don't need anymore." Janet angrily wiped the tears that fell against her will as she drove home. When she arrived home in the driveway, she looked at herself in the car's rear-view mirror and pointed back at herself. "I told you this was gonna happen if you didn't cool it. You done caught feelings for that man and you're not even what he's into," she scolded herself.

Back again in his thoughts, Willie tried to understand what had transpired for her to walk out on him like that. Had he offended her? He knew they joked around a lot. Could it be that he had said anything that crossed her boundaries? Willie thought long and hard, but just couldn't come up with the answer.

Day turned to evening, and as Willie lay on his bed, his thoughts continued to be of Janet. What could have triggered her to act so cold with him? Since they had become so close, there had never been a day when he was without her company. He saw her daily at work. On days he wasn't scheduled to work, he came over to her house in the evenings when she was home. He had indeed missed Janet's company. Willie's thoughts were spinning. It felt like his whole world had been pulled out from underneath him, just from not (really) connecting with Janet for twenty-four hours. It pained Willie that as close as he and Janet were, it seemed the relationship was on the verge of breaking in two before it could ever really officially get started.

Willie shook that thought from his head. Not being in Janet's life was too hard to even think about. It sent his stomach into knots. Willie decided it would be a much happier and stress-free experience for his stomach and heart if he focused on Janet's beauty.

Rubbing his palm over his heart, Willie allowed himself to get lost in his thoughts again. All he could see was Janet's smiling face. He briefly stared out the window. Through the moonlight's glow, the autumn leaves fluttered gracefully to the ground to join a cluster of fallen leaves. These leaves were beautiful but held no comparison to Janet's radiant copper brown skin.

He thought of the time they had been in the mountains, and she'd dropped her glove. When she stood up, her hazel eyes had refracted the sun with a glow. The world seemed to move in slow motion that day, as the kids rambunctiously played in the fields. For a moment, they locked eyes. Janet's electrifying smile touched her eyes and Willie didn't think he'd ever seen anything so beautiful. Some girls needed makeup and overdone hair to elicit the attention of men. But not Janet. Her eyes were everything - trustworthy, alluring, and sweet all at the same time. He could just fall into those eyes. Willie made a secret name for her that day, "Pretty Eyes." From now on, his heart and mind would make the name Pretty Eyes synonymous with Janet.

Willie reflected on the friendly race he had with Janet on the mountain. He had chivalrously let her have a head start to win the race. As he jogged behind her, he couldn't help but notice her hair cascading over her shoulders in tumbles of brown with honey highlights.

Willie finally allowed himself to pursue the one thought of Janet he had pushed aside. Willie thought about what it would be like to kiss her. He imagined her lips had to be satin pillow-soft. Janet was indeed a beautiful woman; he wondered why it had taken him so long to notice. It was as if a bright light had illuminated Willie's heart and mind. Right then and there, he jumped up from his bed with an epiphany. "I'm falling in love with Janet," he openly declared out loud to himself.

"I've got to get her and make her mine."

Just as soon as the epiphany had warmed his heart, the doubts assaulted his mind. He wanted to run to Janet and declare his newfound love for her, but all his doubts and fears told him his feelings wouldn't be reciprocated. Janet only viewed him as a friend. She had mentioned in casual conversation that she wasn't ready to give herself over to a relationship. Her focus was on raising and providing for her kids. Besides, she had been so angry with him at work that day. Cutting him off when he spoke. Reminding him he was her subordinate by giving him that list and purposely avoiding her. No, better not to rush in and admit all of his feelings just yet. Willie decided he would gauge Janet's emotions the next day at work.

Willie noticed Janet's car wasn't in the parking lot the following day at work. As the day pressed on, he realized she wasn't coming. When his shift ended, he made a beeline with his car to Janet's house. Willie didn't have a plan. Whether he would declare his feelings for Janet that day or not, he was unsure of. One thing he was determined about was that day he was going to lay eyes on her.

When Willie pulled up in the driveway, the children greeted him. The kids were excited about his visit. Once inside, Willie took his usual seat at the dining table. Janet sat across from him. He asked her pointedly why she hadn't been to work that day. "Janet, is everything okay? Why have you been so cold towards me? Have I offended you in any way? If so, please know that I'm so sorry. Our friendship means the world to me. I can't stand the thought of you being upset with me. My stomach is in knots."

Willie stared intently into the gleams of Janet's hazel eyes, expecting something. Janet didn't utter a word at first. She drew in a deep breath, and to his surprise, *she* apologized. "No, it's me that should apologize to you, Willie. I've just had a lot going on emotionally and I shouldn't have taken it out on you. I'm so sorry if I hurt you." Not willing to reveal her feelings, she left her explanation vague. *Be cool Janet, you don't want to push him away and lose your friendship,* she coached herself.

"I'll tell you what, it'll all be water under the bridge if you let me take you out for dinner, alone."

"Alone?" Janet asked.

"Yes. We have so much fun with the kids, but I think it's time you let me treat you to a night out."

Janet fought hard to hide her enthusiasm. This felt like she was being asked on a real date. Secretly she was, but only Willie was privy to that information.

"Well, I want to say yes."

"Then why don't you?" Willie asked.

"Let me confirm with my oldest sister, Ruby, if she can babysit. And if she tells me yes, then it's a yes for you as well."

2

LOVE AND MARRIAGE

Janet received a resounding "yes" from Ruby over the telephone. "Girl, you work so hard and even though I know you play hard too, you deserve some alone adult time. Bring my sweet nephews to me ASAP," Ruby said.

Janet dropped the kids off at Ruby's place that Friday. Then Willie drove them to the Sun City Hotel. From conversations before, he already knew it was Janet's favorite place to dine.

Janet took in the blue sky and fresh day as she rode alongside Willie. Every now and again, they would spot some wildflowers growing along the grass near the highway, or find a horse to admire in a farmer's stable. Now that things were set back right with Willie and Janet, the whole world was right and fresh in their hearts. They didn't want to miss anything that could be a memory they would later cherish and discuss. This was, of course, their first official date. (Although Willie was the only one up to date on that piece of secret information, Janet was, of course, hopeful.) She swore to herself she would hide her hand and not be the first one to show that she was holding a pounding heart for him.

The electricity between them threatened to give each one's feelings away as they rode along that day. If Janet saw a horse on Willie's side of the road, she would point it out to him. If Willie saw some wildflowers arrayed in a beautiful color scheme, he would point it out to Janet. This cross action, of course, caused them to glance in each other's eyes constantly and to smile at each other helplessly each time they caught the other.

No matter how hard Janet had fought to just remain friends with Willie and not complicate her life with a man, the cat was out of the bag. She was in love. She just hoped Willie felt the same way too. *He seems like it right now*; she thought to herself. *But I'm so different from the young, pretty, slim girl who came up to see him at work the other day*. Janet sighed in her thoughts.

Finally, they pulled up to the Sun City Hotel. "You knew this was my favorite, didn't you?" Janet smiled at Willie as he held the door open for her.

Willie winked at her as the server walked towards him. "Willie Bell, I called earlier for a quiet table for two."

"Oh yes, Mr. Bell, I have your table ready right this way."

Janet and Willie followed the server, and Willie picked up their conversation. "I think I may remember you telling a story or two of how much fun you'd had here as a teenager."

"Oh, wait one minute now Willie Bell. I mainly came here for the food. I've always been a lady, even if I was a teenage Mama." Janet said this as she playfully tossed one of the beautifully folded duck napkins at him as he held out her seat and she slid in. They both laughed.

"I'll give you both some time to order," the server said, as he headed off to the kitchen.

"Oh shoot, I've dismantled my poor duck napkin. It was so finely put together there's no way I'll be able to put it back together again. I guess I'll just have to admire yours."

"Huh huh. So, while you're staring over here at me, your excuse is you're just looking at "Ducky" right?"

The flirtatious mood was in the air from that point forward.

"Oh stop. Ain't nobody trying to look at you, Mr. Bell."

"I'll tell you what, you continue to admire "ducky" and I'll simply admire you, ok?" Willie asked this with a flirtatious grin.

Janet grabbed the napkin and turned it into an accordion Chinese fan and began dramatically fanning herself. "Can you pass me a menu, please?"

"Of course."

Now that she had created a make-shift fan, Janet had something to block her view of Willie with, otherwise she might reveal too much of her feelings right there on the spot.

Their cuisine order arrived and Janet enjoyed the array of seafood on their table. Her favorite by far were the coconut shrimp and the delicious gourmet fruity tasting dipping sauce that came with them. Nobody made coconut shrimp and dipping sauce like Sun City.

Willie seemed to be engrossed in his filet mignon when he surprised her. "Hey you're having too much fun with that shrimp alone."

Janet stretched the tray out to him. "I can't reach it. Maybe you can feed me a couple." Willie gave her the sweetest puppy dog look and blinked his eyes.

"Oh, of course." Janet smiled. She grabbed a coconut

shrimp and airplaned it over to Willie. Then just before it reached his lips, she pretended to feed Ducky instead. "Oops, sorry, this one is for Ducky." They both broke out into laughter.

After the meal, Willie took Janet's hand in his and told her how much he had fallen in love with her over time and wanted to start a relationship with her. "Janet, I've grown so close to you and your children over the last few months. I don't even know if you realize just how happy you've made me to be a part of your world. But I have to be honest with you, being just friends feels too hard with all the feelings I have inside for you. Well, I'm going on and on. Tell me how you feel."

"Honestly, this *is* surprising. I mean, I was not expecting you to ask me out now to talk of a relationship, but if I'm being completely honest, it's a nice surprise,"Janet said. She gazed into Willie's chocolate eyes with deep intention. "Listen Willie, I've been hurt in the past and it really tore me down. I have two kids to raise and I can't afford to be broken-hearted and not fully present for them."

"Wait. Listen Janet. I see the dedicated woman you are to your children and I love the woman that you are all around -"

Janet cut him off. "I wish I could believe that, but it's just unimaginable that as handsome as you are you would choose me."

"Sweetheart, what is unimaginable about a man asking a beautiful woman who has been his best friend and heart to accept his commitment in exchange for hers?"

Deep inside, Janet wanted this, but she was scared. She began making excuses. "It's just that I thought we only wanted a relationship that was built on pure friendship, Willie."

"In the beginning, I wanted friendship, but now I want something more; I want an exclusive, intimate relationship with you, perhaps even marriage," Willie responded as he leaned in, meeting Janet's eyes and anticipating her response.

She seemed so confused then and glanced at Willie, who was making straight eye contact for a reply by then.

"Well, are you in any relationship already? We have been friends and you've never mentioned that to me." His tone seemed to turn dark.

Janet's eyes opened wide. Instinctively, she became defensive and let out the question that had been holding her back from committing to Willie. "I am not in any relationship. Are you? Because you seemed chummy with that pretty young lady you were talking to at work last week."

"What girl? Wait, do you mean my niece Maya? Is that why you were upset with me?"

"Maybe," Janet said, feeling both foolish and relieved to hear that it was his niece.

Slowly, both of them let smiles and laughter erupt. "Janet, I had promised my niece to contribute to her prom, that's why she was there, to pick some money up."

"Oh." Janet blushed. Now I'm embarrassed.

"There's no need for you to be embarrassed. As a matter of fact, you're really cute when you're jealous."

"Oh, stop!" Janet pouted.

"No, you really are. I wish you could see yourself, Janet. I really do. The way I do. You're a beautiful woman inside and out. I meant what I said earlier. I want an exclusive and intimate relationship with you. I love your kids and I already know in my heart one day I'll ask you to marry me and we'll continue building our family."

"I've been so focused on being a single mother and

raising my kids that I pushed out the notion of having a dream of my own. Secretly, I've been holding back my feelings for you, but now that I know you have a family man's plan for us, I would love to get started on that journey with you. It would be my greatest dream to complete a family with you," Janet replied.

The two friends had now taken an enormous step and their relationship had finally surpassed friendship to a relationship they hoped to build a future on. Things were looking promising. Their path of closeness grew. Willie wasn't raised in church but he began accompanying Janet and the children to her church. Eventually, they aligned socially and spiritually and started planning a future together.

Two years later...

One evening on bended knee, Willie pulled out a ring and asked Janet to marry him. "Janet, we've been dating for two years now. I know beyond a shadow of a doubt that I never want to be without you. Will you marry me?"

This was everything Janet had ever hoped for, but yet she hesitated. What about her family and friends? What would they say when they found out she was to be married? No one outside of work even knew she was dating anyone. Janet had been incredibly secretive about her relationship with Willie. She would at least need to speak with someone in the family about this.

Janet's hesitation was **not** the reaction Willie had been hoping for. Here he was ready to spend his whole life with her, step up and be a father figure to her two boys and have some children of their own someday. *Here I am trying to do things the right way and this is her reaction?*

Willie's eyebrows narrowed and that same dark look came over him that Janet had seen when she hesitated to think things over after his invitation for a close relationship two years ago. Could there be a different side to Willie?

"Wow Janet. Nothing? Well, do you want to get married or not?" His tone was harsh.

Janet found herself trying to ease his irritation. "Baby, of course I want to marry you. It's just... I want to talk with my family first. I haven't included them in on our relationship and I think it's about time I did." Janet truly wanted to marry him but she could only imagine the shock all of this was going to send to her close-knit family.

Willie composed himself as he and Janet sat down at the dining room table across from each other. He didn't like to feel like he was begging. But he decided to see things from her perspective, knowing she was close to her family.

"WELL, in the meantime, baby, can I slip this ring on your finger?"

"Yes, of course you can. And of course, I'll marry you. I just want to talk with my family first."

"Okay sweetheart, I understand, but don't make me wait too long. I don't want this to be a long engagement. We can head down to the courthouse tomorrow from my perspective." Willie said.

"How about next week?" Janet asked.

"Next week is perfect," Willie said as he smoothed the side of Janet's hair and slowly kissed her goodnight.

The next day, on a lunch date with her sister Ruby, Janet revealed to her sister that she had been in a long-term relationship with Willie. You could have knocked Ruby over with a feather from the reaction she gave. Her mouth dropped. "Getting married! Married to who? Ain't no man asked Daddy for your hand in marriage. Look Janet, I think it's beautiful and all that you've found love, but how much do you know about this guy?"

"What do you mean, Ruby? We work together and we've been dating for the past two years."

"Then why haven't we met him? At least Mama and Daddy. Janet, there is something suspicious about a man you don't feel comfortable bringing around your family, not even your parents, for two years. Listen sis, I love you and I want the best for you. My advice is to wait and marry him after the family gets to know him a little. Let Daddy and Mama meet him and have a nice dinner with him, find out about his background a little."

"I understand what you're saying, sis, but Willie is in a hurry to get married. He's waited two years and I don't want to make him wait any longer."

"It's your decision, Janet, but I'm not in agreement with it," Ruby said.

Immediately after her lunch with Janet, Ruby reached out to her parents. They had the same reservations she did. Janet's parents called Janet and told her they thought she should wait. Not wanting to argue, she hurriedly got off the phone with them. In her heart, she knew she would do what Willie suggested and not them.

The following week the two got married. They had a courthouse wedding attended by family members, close friends, and employees at the restaurant. After Willie and Janet tied the knot, they moved into an apartment together in Center Point (a suburb of Birmingham). But don't let the word "suburb" fool you. Center Point was rough. And the apartment complex their credit and income could afford them was particularly rough. Gangs and drugs were rampant. Once the children were jumped on their way home from walking to the store. And the upstairs neighbor was found killed execution style most likely by a Mexican Cartel. Janet couldn't help but hope her family would be safe.

3

REAL LIFE

E ight years later...

IN HIGH SCHOOL, Adreion Shaw joined the Center Point high school football team. He had enjoyed playing football ever since he was a child; he was a fantastic putter. Adreion acquired this craft from his grandfather William Shaw, Janet's father, who worked so hard on what's called "reading greens." This is when you hustle and work hard on the football field.

Adreion loved football because it made him feel the sunshine on his shoulders while completing a challenge and enjoying a day with his friends. Also, it gave him a good core workout that increased his strength. Adreion had no idea just how life saving his strength training would turn out to be.

～

AFTER THE BIRTH of Janet's youngest son Willie Bell jr., episodes of dark events unfolded. The procedure of filing income taxes had become an issue between Janet and Willie. Every year they would disagree on who would claim the children as dependents on their taxes. This yearly argument began to stretch past tax season and leak over into the rest of the year, with Willie holding resentment that he couldn't force Janet's hand.

The biggest debate surrounded the money that could be gained as a tax refund by claiming dependents. Normally this wouldn't have been a problem if the couple had filed taxes the legal way, which is Married Filing Jointly. But after marriage, the two continued to file individual single taxes, with each claiming head of household seeking a refund for dependents.

After the birth of Willie Bell jr., they made an agreement to file taxes as a couple. Janet wanted to file income taxes the legal way (as a married couple). Even though Willie made an agreement on the way they were to file, when tax season rolled around again, he fought against it. "I should be able to file my own taxes with my own son on them and receive the refund since I take care of him."

Willie wasn't the only one changing up on agreements either. Throughout the six years Janet and Willie had been married, Janet had gone back and forth on her stance to file taxes as a married couple. After having Willie Jr, juggling three children and a job became a little more than Janet could handle for a time. Oftentimes Janet was late to work and missed days taking care of Willie Jr. until eventually they let her go. When this happened, she was more than willing to file taxes separately because, according to her tax calculations, it was more beneficial. But when Janet would pick up a job in a year and she and Willie had similar incomes, she would again insist that they file as a couple, because from her understanding of the tax code, that would be more financially beneficial during that time.

Janet also agreed to file separately when she wasn't working so that she could claim single status with the government and collect more food stamps for her and her children. This mixed messaging confused Willie. When people hear marriages can be destroyed because of money, they probably don't think of these scenarios in detail. The bible says the love of money is the root of all kinds of evil. And evil was building.

Of course, both Janet and Willie had their rationalizations for why each of them held their convictions. Janet was just trying to do what would bring in the most money to take care of the children. Willie, on the other hand, felt threatened by Janet's higher income whenever she did work. He felt this was what gave her the gall to want to take the lead in the financial decision making of their marriage. This gnawed at his ego like a dog chewing on a bone. Eventually, the pain was going to come out in some form or fashion.

One time, when Janet wasn't working, Willie had income and Janet didn't. She gave in and let Willie file all the children as head of household and receive a large income tax refund in his name. All that year it had become increasingly difficult to ease the frustrations of Willie as he was not used to paying so many of the bills and frankly couldn't handle it. It turned him into that dark person she had only seen glimpses of during their time dating. Willie would become loud and grab Janet by the face in the middle of disagreements, especially about money.

Tax years became increasingly more violent. One year, when Janet did not have any income, Willie claimed all the children and received a huge income tax refund check. This became a problem because they did not split the check-in half. They both wanted more than the other.

This began the culmination of the sorrows to come.

"You're gonna do what I say. I'm the man of this house," Willie yelled as he tossed Janet across the room and against the wall."

"Don't touch my mama," Javari yelled.

Willie backhanded him for speaking out of turn.

"Willie, stop! Please!" Janet begged.

Willie was all riled up now. There was no stopping him. He punched Janet in the face.

"Don't touch my mother!" Adreion yelled as he charged Willie like he was an opponent to be taken down.

It surprised Willie how much strength Adreion had. It took his attention off Janet for a time. He realized going head to head with him wasn't something he wanted to do right there and then. Also, Willie Jr. had begun screaming and crying. This seemed to jar him back into reality from wherever he had zoned off to in his head. *Oh no, what have I done?* Willie asked himself. He looked at Janet slumped against the wall with blood on her face. Bruises had begun to appear. The children encircled around her, trying to comfort her. Adreion had wet a towel to help her clean up.

Willie didn't know how he could apologize. Why couldn't Janet just let him be the man of the house like he should be? He thought. *This would have never happened if she would have just let me run things*, he thought to himself. Willie had always had an anger problem, but he could usually keep it at bay when a woman knew how to listen. He mulled over his relationship with Janet and the children in his mind. *A lot of men wouldn't even marry a heavyset woman with extra kids. Here I am trying to be a family man and she won't let me. She should treat me better, anyway.* Those last thoughts helped relieve Willie of the responsibility and guilt he was feeling for how he had treated Janet and the children and with that in a cocky tone he announced, "Man, I ain't got to take this. I'm out."

Everyone in the home was relieved that Willie had left, except little Willie and secretly Janet, too. Immediately, she felt guilty about the money, but at the same time, she knew she was just trying to do what was best for her family. Would Willie return? Never could she have imagined that the sweet man who asked for her heart at Sun City Hotel and later for her hand in marriage would turn out to be this way.

Janet breathed a sigh of relief when income tax season was over and Willie returned. Willie Jr., was the only one who seemed slightly agreeable to forgiving him. Although he never asked for forgiveness, it was just implied that it would happen when Janet welcomed Willie back home.

The children had seen Willie become progressively worse every tax season. "Mama, can we just stop filing taxes?" Willie Jr. asked.

"Oh baby." Janet reached out and gave Willie Jr. a hug. "I wish it were that simple."

"He's a monster." Adreion told his mother one day when Willie wasn't home.

"Don't say that, Adreion. It's just hard for him taking care of everyone and paying all the bills by himself during the times I don't work. Things are going to get better, you'll see." Janet hoped she was telling her children the truth. She could only hope.

Javari and Adreion had already had their own conversation about the matter. "I can't stand him," Javari said.

"Me either," Adreion replied. "But I know one thing: I'll be ready for him the next time."

"You think he's gonna cut up again when taxes come?"

"Don't worry about it - like I said, brother, I'm ready for him."

Whenever income tax was brought up, Willie would become aggressive and end up physically abusing Janet. This kind of behavior made the kids dislike him. Javari and Adreion always liked Willie when he was dating their mother. In fact, they loved him - until living with him day to day unveiled that he had turned out to be a monster. There was just no going back to the old relationship with him at this point. Not after the physical altercations they'd had with him while trying to protect their mother. Their stepfather had displayed his true nature.

All three of the boys knew their mama's house rule, *what happens in this house stays in this house*. Adreion was gearing himself up with training to handle the task of protecting the family on his own. Javari wanted to tell someone but decided to keep their family's household secret. But Willie Jr. was young. This rule wasn't as deeply ingrained in him as his siblings. And even though he was Willie's only biological child in the house, the abuse had even surpassed Willie Jr.'s love and loyalty to his father. Willie Jr. reached out and complained about what was going on in the house to his grandmother.

While cleaning the house one day, Janet received an unexpected visit from her mother, Mary. Mary's look was intense from the moment she walked through the door. "Look, Janet, I need to discuss something with you." Janet and her mother sat at the dining room table. "Janet, has Willie been putting his hands on you? Now don't you lie to me." Janet took three quick breaths in. She knew she couldn't lie to her mother - her face, voice, and body language would betray her. Her heart was pounding. *How did Mama know?*

"Mama, where would you get that from?"

"Don't you worry about where I got that from. I'm a mother and a grandmother on a mission today. And I want you and my grandchildren safe."

Janet fought back tears. She had to be strong. "Mama, me and Willie ain't going through nothing nobody else hasn't gone through in marriage. I'm fine, okay."

"Janet, I'm concerned about you and the kids. Honey, being worried about your safety is not a regular thing you should get used to and think that's just a part of marriage, because it's not. You understand me, baby?"

"Yes Mama, I understand."

"Good. Well, hear me well. I believe marriage is for a lifetime, but it shouldn't threaten to snuff out your life. If things are getting dangerous, then baby, you may have to separate or even divorce."

Janet looked at her mother in disbelief. Oh, she had heard this before from the officers who had come over when things had gotten out of hand between her and Willie, but she never expected to hear her mother (the woman who had been married to her father for decades) mention divorce. Mary caught Janet's shocked stare. "Honey, I want you and these children safe and I believe God does, too. Your children need you."

"I know, Mama, but we're just going through a temporary spell." Mary blew her breath and cocked her head to one side. She brushed Janet's arm with her hand, trying to express genuine concern without being too pushy.

She had gotten through to Janet. Mary could see a grain of acceptance in Janet's eyes. Mary was a woman that didn't push her opinions on her adult children. So Janet had to know if her mama was being this bold with her words, it was coming from a place of pure wisdom and love.

Janet reflected on the last time the police were called to their apartment because of a domestic disturbance. Once Willie knew the police were on their way, he had gotten out of dodge before they could get there. When the police arrived, Janet was sobbing and bloody from Willie laying his hands on her.

Once, Police Sergeant Red had been among the police that answered the call. Willie jr. recognized him from a visit he and the chief had done at their school. He had gotten to turn on the siren in Red's car and meet the police dog, Big Ben.

"Hey Sergeant Red. Where's the Chief and Big Ben?"

"Hey there, little buddy," Red responded. "Well, you know, the chief only comes out for the big stuff. Talking with your Mama is something they let me handle all on my own." Red and Willie Jr. chuckled.

"What about Big Ben?"

"We mostly bring old Big Ben out when there's something to sniff, otherwise he's somewhere with his legs kicked back, watching his favorite game show and eating a steak." The whole family had to laugh at that one.

The police took the statement of the children and Janet that day. She didn't want to press charges. "He's gone now, officers. I don't want to press charges, I just want to keep me and my children safe."

Sergeant Red took Janet aside from the children. "Listen, we've had some laughs tonight, but all joking aside, I understand you're saying you feel safe for you and your children now, because he's gone, but is it going to stay that way?"

"Sergeant Red, Willie hasn't always been like this. We were a loving couple when we first met and the children loved him. Somehow, with the pressures of life in our years of marriage, he changed."

"That's often the way it is with these situations, Janet. I've seen a lot of domestic violence situations in my line of work and from my experience, they often progress to something too evil to mention. If the woman and children make it out alive, it's usually at a huge cost to their mental health."

Now listen, Janet, I'm not trying to overstep my bounds here. I'm really not, but you've got not only you to think about but those kids and your mental and physical ability to take care of them. And as a mother, your number one job is to protect them - all of them. Now if I hear anything else about him putting his hands on one of these kids, I'm going to have to arrest him rather you want to press charges or not, you understand?"

"Yes sir, I understand," Janet replied.

"Well look here, I'm supposed to report what's been going on here to Children Services, but if you tell me you're going to keep Willie out of the house and away from these kids, I'll take your word for it."

"Sergeant Red, you don't have to worry about me or the children. I won't let Willie darken my doorstep again."

"Okay, so just so we're clear now - you will be separating or divorcing from Willie Bell?"

"We will be separating for sure."

"Alright now. Y'all be safe and if you need the number of a good lawyer, let me know, you here."

"I will. Thank you, Sergeant Red."

Janet was always quick to have tender feelings for Willie in her heart again after every episode they had, but this time she knew something had to change. Sergeant Red had mentioned Child Services, and losing her children was not something she was willing to do.

It's just I've held on so tightly to the memory of who Willie was, waiting for that loving man I fell in love with to return. And I've tried to humble myself to my husband for the sake of the children and our marriage, but God I want me and my kids to be alright. I wish it could be that way with Willie here, but unfortunately right now it can not.

Janet thought long and hard as she sat on the edge of her bed staring at Willie's name on her phone before hitting the dial button. Janet knew marriage was not always a bed full of roses. It has its own thorns and turning points. She wasn't ready to decide her marriage should be over for good because it could have a good turning point in the future.

Janet rehearsed what she would say and called Willie. To her surprise, Willie was agreeable. They both thought it would be wiser for them to separate rather than to divorce. Secretly, Janet hoped the Willie she fell in love with would one day return.

They separated, and the glow was back as the family was happy once again. Giggles could be heard in the neighborhood through the corners of the wall. Janet was satisfied as before, even without Willie - to her surprise - ESPECIALLY without Willie. When Janet and Willie were together, down through the years, it's like she somehow had locked herself in. Her home and even her mind had become a secret cage or dungeon that she couldn't let anyone into or they might see the truth, that she and her children were no longer a family in the true sense of the word with Willie, but his domestic violence victims. They were subjects to the whims of his anger.

Now with Willie gone, everyone in the home felt freer, especially Janet. Now she could talk with her friends and family again. Now she wasn't suffocating under abuse. Being free had its perks, but deep down, she was a broken woman.

During the day Janet would put on a strong, brave, happy face, but in her alone time she would sit in the bathtub with tears rolling down her cheeks, wishing for her happy family back again. "Why would a relationship built up for ten years just fade away?" Janice asked these questions of herself out loud as she looked into a hand-held mirror while soaking in the tub.

She had a habit of romanticizing the past 10 years whenever Willie was out of the home. They had made *this* separation official, something they had never done before. And even though ultimately it was Janet's hope that Willie would agree amicably to a separation for the sake of the children, she was mighty surprised when he did. She thought he would have fought harder and argued to stay. But no, he just simply agreed. "Am I not beautiful to him anymore?" She asked the reflection staring back at her.

Janet set the mirror down and leaned back in the tub to relax. She looked up at the ceiling as she processed her thoughts. *I wish things could be different with me and Willie. Why would a man who has been my best friend, my love, and even my colleague inflict so much pain on my heart and body?*

Janet used a bristle body brush and rubbed shay cleansing oil on her arms, legs, and body. She moved slowly, massaging thoughts out loud as she pampered her skin. "Maybe this is something Willie can't help and needs counseling for, or did he do this to me purposely? Does his quick agreement to move out mean he no longer adores me like before?"

Janet realized she had begun soliloquizing. She had done this since she was a teenager. Speaking her thoughts out loud helped her retrace her steps anytime she lost focus.

On the day Willie was scheduled to come and get his

things while the kids were in school, he surprised Janet. He was humble. "Baby, please forgive me. I just want to make things right with us. Please let me come home to you and the kids. If I take my things away from here -"

Willie bent over in sobs. "Janet, baby, if I take my things away from here, I just feel we won't find our way back to each other and it won't be temporary. Baby, I should have never hurt you or the kids. Please forgive me. I promise you I can be the man you once loved again. Do you remember the way we used to laugh and the fun we used to have on the mountain with the kids?"

Willie caressed Janet's face. She winced. Her cheek bone was still sore from days before when he hurt her. She realized she still held some resentment for how he hurt her and the kids, but it wasn't enough to erase his hold on her. She still loved him. *Look how vulnerable he's being right now, she thought to herself.*

Despite everything, maybe even her better judgment, Janet decided to forgive Willie Bell, who had asked for forgiveness to make things right. Many voices of decision were in her head, her mother's, her sister's, hers - especially her emotions. Look at this handsome man whom she had pledged her life to humbling himself for her. He had cried and everything. Wouldn't she be a bad person if she didn't forgive her husband and accept him back, especially after he had accepted the responsibility and admitted he had hurt her and the children and said he felt remorse?

"Janet, please let me make amends. Let me come home to you and the children."

"Let me call my pastor for advice," Janet told Willie.

The pastor spoke with both Willie and Janet. After that, they agreed to reconcile. "Willie, let me just give the kids some time to heal and I'll have you come on back home."

"How long, Janet, a couple of days?"

"Let's try for a week."

"Okay. I'll see you soon."

A week later, Janet broke the news to her son Adreion that Willie would return. Janet had assured him they had solved their issues and set aside their disagreements and problems to focus on the family's well-being. Adreion listened to his mother out of respect, but inside he was devastated. He felt resentful towards Willie Bell returning to their lives, especially after he had caused his mother so much pain.

Adreion did not want him coming back and living under the same roof as them, but ultimately, it was his mother's decision. He reflected on the talk he and his mother had had before she decided to reconcile with Willie. They had plans to move into another house. "Just Us." She had said.

Janet's plans had changed, but Adreion's hadn't. He kept his old plan in the back of his mind. *Be ready for anything.* He knew his mom was forgiving because of her emotional ties to her husband, but there was no way Willie Bell had changed. Willie had been in his life for over a decade now and lived with him, his mom, and his brothers. Over the years, Adreion and Willie got into physical altercations because he tried to protect his mother. He'd seen too much to expect a change out of this man, even if his mother did hope for it.

One week later...

JANET'S YOUNGER SISTER, Iesha, had a dream that her mother killed her father over some money. She awoke and immediately looked for her father to make sure her mother had not, in fact, killed him. Thank goodness everyone in her home was safe. But the dream was so real. Iesha knew it had some sort of prophetic meaning.

Iesha also knew that the person you dream about is often a representation of the actual people involved. She believed it was a message about someone very close to her. Someone in her family. She called each of her sisters that morning, starting with the eldest, Ruby, and then Tameika.

"Are you on bad terms with your husband?" She asked each of them. Both gave her a resounding "No."

Next, Iesha checked in with her siblings, Earnest and Michelle. Even though neither of them were married, she wanted to cover her bases. This dream was too vivid. It was a warning. It was definitely someone close to her.

Finally, Iesha phoned Janet. She had been last on her list, since she knew Janet had separated from Willie to keep her and the children safe. "Janet, is Willie back there at the house?"

"Girl, no, you know I put him out." Janet had the phone on speaker as she was fixing the children's breakfast for school. She eyed the children as she said this.

"Okay, well, I had a crazy dream, so I was just checking in on y'all," Iesha said.

As everyone in Janet's home was preparing to leave for school, she gave the children a quick reminder. "Now you remember everything that happens in this house stays in this house, right?"

"Yes Mama," the children all said in unison.

"Okay. Just so we're clear, y'all know my policy. Everyone should get them some business and mind it. And our business is not anyone else's. I don't care who it is. Right?"

Little Willie shook his head in agreement. "Right Mama."

"Yes ma'am," Adreion agreed. Javari was not there. He had gone to stay with his Aunt Ruby for a little while.

Something about Janet's answer just didn't sit well with Iesha. She knew Janet was an extremely private person. *Is it possible my sister's not telling me the truth?* She thought to herself. "I've got to get to the bottom of this dream. It was definitely a message." Iesha spoke this aloud as she dialed Janet's cell phone. She hoped one of the kids would answer, as they sometimes did when Janet was busy fixing dinner.

Adreion answered and she asked him pointedly, "Adreion, is Willie Bell back staying with y'all?"

Adreion paused. He wanted to tell his aunt the truth, but

his mother was standing right there and she had already warned him this morning. His thoughts reflected on what she had said, "What happens in this house stays in this house. It's our business."

"No ma'am, auntie, he's not back," Adreion lied.

"Let me speak to Willie jr.," Iesha said.

"He's not home from school yet," Adreion said.

"Okay, well, when he gets in, I want you to have him call me."

"Alright I will auntie."

When Willie Jr. came, Janet gave him a prompt reminding of her words from that morning. "Your Aunt Iesha wants you to call her. Don't forget when you talk to anybody to keep our business private."

Willie nodded.

Janet knew Willie Jr. was young and subject to let the cat out of the bag if pressed too hard with questions, so she placed the phone on speaker as he made the phone call. To Willie Jr.'s surprise, his grandma answered the phone. None of them had ever lied to Grandma Mary.

"Hey baby, Mary's warm voice could be heard over the phone."

Willie Jr. was excited at the sound of his grandma's voice. "Hey grandma, I love you."

"I love you too, sweetheart."

Mary checked in with Willie jr. on how school was going and about his homework. "Have you been doing your reading?"

"Oh yes ma'am," he said.

"Alright now, let me speak with your big brother."

"I'm right here, grandma," Adreion responded.

Mary decided it wouldn't be right to involve Willie Jr. since he was a younger child, so she directed her question to

Adreion. She asked him flat out. "Adreion, has Willie Bell been coming around there? Or is he back in the house with y'all?"

Janet paused when she heard the question posed to Adreion. She gave him a look that said, "Remember what I said earlier!"

Adreion felt the only way to respect his mother in that moment was to lie to his grandma, so he did. "No ma'am, it's just us and Mama staying here now."

Mary drew a sigh of relief. "Okay. Thank you, sweetheart. Now y'all finish your chores up and help your mama around the house, okay?"

"Alright grandma, love you."

"Love you grandma," Willie jr. chimed in.

Iesha blessed each of the children over the phone, and then they all hung up. And the lie hung in the air, because Willie **was** in the house and Adreion did not tell Aunt Iesha or Grandma the truth. Iesha and Mary were at a false peace that all was well in Janet's home and put the dream aside.

The truth was that within a couple of days of Willie Bell's return, his repentant heart had evaporated. In fact, the return of Willie Bell had meant the return of chaos and drama. Arguments could be heard through the paper-thin apartment walls. Neighbors didn't know what to do. Now that Willie was back, Janet was no longer free inside and retreated within herself again and once again act distant with her friends and neighbors.

While the kids were at school one day, somehow that old argument about income tax money resurfaced. Willie began getting aggressive with Janet during the argument. He grabbed her and shoved her against the wall, holding her by her shoulders while he panted.

As his breath was hitting her face, she watched his eyes

bulge with fury. That's when Janet realized it had been a mistake to ever let Willie Bell back in. There was a knock at the door and Willie let go of his grip on Janet. They both walked to the door and it was a package delivery Janet needed to sign for. Janet quickly signed. She was visibly shaken.

"Are you alright ma'am?" The delivery driver asked.

Janet saw this as her chance to have a witness around that Willie wouldn't cut up in front of, so despite her pride, she held the door wide open while the delivery driver stood there and said. "I will be. You need to leave, now Willie!"

The delivery driver stood there uncomfortably as Willie Jr. left the house fussing under his breath. "Are you sure you're alright, ma'am? Can I call someone for you?" The delivery driver asked.

"No, I'm fine. He's gone now, everything's alright."

"Okay, you be safe now." And with that, the delivery driver departed.

Willie called Janet on the cell phone. "What was that slick stuff you did, putting me out in front of the delivery driver?"

"Look Willie, it wasn't no slick stuff. You've got to go. I tried to give you a chance and you hurt me again. You haven't changed. I can't have you here with me and the kids. That's it."

"So you're saying it's over?"

"Yes, Willie. It's over! I've had it. I'm done. I have to think about me and my kids."

"Your kids? What about MY son? Huh?" Willie removed the phone from his ear and squeezed it in anger, while looking at the screensaver he had with Janet and the children. He screamed into the phone while stroking Janet and

Willie's part of the picture. "So, what about my son? Huh? Are you just going to keep me from my son?"

"Look Willie, the things that you have been doing aren't safe for me or ANY of the kids, including Willie Jr. I can't talk to you right now." And with that, Janet hung up in Willie's face. She was so drained from all the emotional toil with Willie and the pain from him hemming her up in the corner earlier. She just wanted a little rest before the children came home from school. Janet laid down on her bed to rest.

Little did she know that Willie had never gone far when she put him out of the house. He went for a short walk and began lurking around outside of the apartment. The sliding glass window in Janet's apartment was cracked just enough for him to slide it open and get inside.

In a blaze of fury, Willie hollered for Janet and heard her make startled movements in the bed. He made a beeline for the bedroom and choked Janet as she was lying down. She had made this final. Anger had engulfed him. He choked her with all his might, saying, "You're going to take me away from my son." He kept choking her until the last breath was out of her body and her lifeless body lain there dead.

Next, he hid in the closet until Adreion came home. When Adreion got home, he noticed the house was unusually quiet. His mom normally would buzz around stirring dinner pots or setting out snacks for them. Adreion looked in the kitchen. He knocked on the bathroom door, but there was no sign of his mother. The house was completely quiet. Too quiet.

Adreion went to his bedroom to put down his book bag and when he came into the living room, he noticed a closet door open that had not been opened earlier. His eyes veered into his mother's bedroom. From where he was standing in the living room, he could see her lying on the bed. *She must be asleep,* Adreion thought. Adreion knew his mother worked hard around the house, so he decided to let her have her rest. He could fix a snack for himself and for Willie jr. when he got home. *Let me just close the door so Mama can have some peace and quiet,* he thought.

As Adreion got closer to the door, he noticed red all over his mother's beautiful white comforter set. He ran over to where Janet was and saw blood and foam around her face and mouth. "Wake up Mama." Adreion began shaking Janet profusely trying to wake her up. "Mama, please. Mama, please wake up. Wake up, Mama." His voice cracked with every plea until the final realization hit him. His mother was lifeless, and something was terribly wrong.

"This can't be happening," Adreion said frantically. He tried to keep a calm head. "Maybe they can revive Mama." He just needed to find her phone to call 911, so he walked over and turned on the light in the bedroom to get a better view. That's when Willie jumped out of the closet with an extension cord in his hand and started coming towards him.

He lurched for Adreion, but Adreion was too fast for him. He couldn't make it out of the room though and Willie finally cornered him. Adreion had been working out and preparing to protect himself and his mother the next time Willie tried to hurt them. He just wished he had been there to help his mother.

With Adreion cornered, Willie attempted to punch him in the face. Adreion blocked some of the punches and some landed. He had a battle going on in his mind. Should he fight back or just wait for his mom to put Willie out for good once she comes to? Later when interviewed he would tell officers and news media "I didn't want to get in trouble with my mom, so I didn't try to fight him at first." (Subconsciously Adreion knew Janet was gone, but his conscious mind just wouldn't let him process that as reality.)

Willie somehow got behind Adreion and put the cord around his neck. That's when Adreion became hysterical. He kept yelling for his mom. "Mama, help. Mama wake up and help me. Get him off me. Mama, please." But she did not come to help. Janet lay lifeless on her beautiful white bedspread.

Fight or flight kicked in for Adreion, along with all of his training. He decided if he didn't do something NOW he would die. Adreion Shaw fought with all of his might to get out of Willie Bell's grasp and he did. He began punching Willie with mighty blows. At first, Adreion and Willie were standing toe to toe with each other. Each one holding his own in the fight. They knocked each other around until they were in the hallway of the house. They fought for several minutes until finally Adreion's training and youth began to get the best of Willie as Adreion delivered his blows faster and with much more force than Willie could hold.

He knocked Willie off his feet for a moment. That's when Adreion took the opportunity to run out of the front door and escape. He ran to a friend's house in a neighboring apartment, beating on the door for help. While he was beating on the door, a neighbor called down from an upstairs apartment, "What's going on?"

"He's trying to kill me." Adreion replied.

I'll call the police, the neighbor lady said, just as Adreion's friend opened the door and let him in. "Come out here, Adreion. Get out here." Willie could be heard screaming for the teen to come back as he stood outside the door.

"Hey, leave that boy alone. The neighbor lady said."

That's when some of the men in the apartment complex started coming outside. "What's going on?" they asked.

"You know little Adreion? Well, he just came through here running saying Willie Bell was trying to kill him. He went into his friend's apartment and then Willie stood outside the door still threatening him."

"Where is he now?" They asked. "Wait, I see him," one of them answered the other as Willie ran towards Janet's apartment. Three of the men ran after him inside of the apartment and held him down. They called others that lived in the complex to come and help.

The neighbor lady went next door to Adreion's friend's apartment. "It's okay. Y'all can come out. The men out here have him. They're gonna hold him until the police come."

Adreion and his friend went together back inside of Janet's apartment where several men were holding Willie Bell down until the Sheriff and police could get there.

EVERY MONDAY AND FRIDAY, Iesha Shaw and Mary Shaw spent the day washing and grocery shopping. This Monday was no different. On that fateful day, Mary and Iesha left the house and went to the laundromat in town, then bought groceries. They had no clue that Janet had been slain; neither had it dawned on Iesha that the woman in question from her dream was Janet.

Back home, their phone was literally ringing off the hook, with no response. Adreion had called Tameika with grave news and she desperately needed to reach both of them to deliver it.

Next, Tameika tried Iesha on her cell phone and she picked up. "Hello, hello."

"Hello Iesha." Tameika's words sounded like a robot to Iesha on the other end.

"Shoot. Mama, I always have trouble with this phone in Walmart," she told Mary.

Iesha's cell reception was often terrible. "Man, I really need to upgrade my cell phone!" She said.

"Don't worry about it. We'll be home soon," Mary responded.

Finally, when they made it home, Iesha reached Tameika, only to receive the grave news that Willie Bell had killed Janet. Their mother was so shocked that her left eye began twitching nonstop.

Somehow, Mary gathered herself enough to call her husband at work. "William, Janet is dead. Our daughter's gone," she cried into the phone.

William Shaw left work immediately to be with his family. He had no idea how Janet had died. When he arrived home, Mary told him the whole grim tale.

Janet's father, mother, and Iesha all left for Center Point to go get Janet's children. At one point, William pulled over to the side of the road, wiping his tears and trying to catch his breath.

"You alright Daddy?" Iesha asked from the back.

"I feel like I just had the wind knocked out of me."

"Are you alright to be driving?" Mary asked.

"I'll be fine. I've got to get us over there. I can make it."

By the time they made it to the apartment, the police had swept it for evidence and had Willie Bell in handcuffs on the porch. The police had brought Adreion back to go over details in the apartment. They hugged him tightly.

"Where's Willie Jr.?"

"He's gone with the nice social work lady," the chief said. But now that you're here, I'll have them double on back."

The chief phoned Sabrina Bobay. "Ms. Bobay, can you come on back here with Willie Jr.? The family is here now."

Ms. Bobay made it back with Willie jr. and they all headed to Ruby's to meet up with Javari, so all the boys could be together. Everyone was in shock at what had happened. When the family gathered together at Ruby's house, some were quietly dismayed and others were over-come with loud sobs and cries of grief.

Everyone felt the stripping of Janet's life being snuffed out too soon. The autumn leaf had fallen, and Willie Bell was the reason for it. It seemed like everything was happening so fast; it was overwhelming.

Because this was such a heinous crime, it was all over the news and in the papers. The news spread everywhere. People in town and nearby were constantly calling the phone numbers of the family. Some offered comfort, some were trying to get information to pass along. The Shaw family just tried to take it one day at a time.

Iesha and Mary Shaw busied themselves with the arrangements for the funeral. They called family members that were out of town, prepared the meal for after church and Ruby picked out a lovely pink dress to lay Janet to rest in. The funeral came and went. The family cared for the children and continued to just try to take it one day at a time.

After a few weeks, the phone calls slowed down. The visits came to a halt and the family was left alone with their thoughts and memories. As Iesha and Mary were sitting in the living room watching the news, Mr. Shaw was reading the evening paper. "You know, the news is so horrible some-times. But it's a hard pill to swallow when it hits so close to home." With that, he flipped another page and said, "When you make your bed hard, you sleep in it." Everyone knew this was in reference to Janet. He said this because Janet was smart but would not finish college and complete her education. She could have had a whole different life. A better life. She would have had better prospects in life for a husband, job, and home - if she would have made better decisions in her life.

THE REGRETS OF A HUSBAND

James 4:2 Ye lust, and have not: ye kill, and desire to have, and cannot obtain: ye fight and war, yet ye have not, because ye ask not.

SIX YEARS IS MORE than a reasonable length of time to reflect on one's life, but not long enough to pay for irreparable damages. It's taken me that long to fully come to grips with what I have done. Some have claimed that we in jail are more than our greatest mistake; our life cannot and should not be defined by a single blunder, a single poor act, especially if it was eternally regretted. But the truth is that I **am** judging myself for this behavior, as I should. My sense of self, my identity, is undeniably linked to the events of that day six years ago.

I see a man in his fifties in the mirror, still fit and healthy but well into his second half of life, graying around the edges. A nice man who is capable of self-reflection. Newly passionate about reading, a consumer of information, a good communicator, a good cook, and a good laugher. I see a brother, a friend, a Father and a son. I also see a young man who killed the lady he loved for money and control. I choked her, leaving a puddle of blood on the bed. That's undeniable.

My name is Willie Bell. That's what I did. That's what I did to a lady I said was the love of my life and the center of my universe. I couldn't let her go; I'd rather she die a violent death than continue to live without me. Instead of me asking Jesus to be my Lord and help me change my ways from being abusive, controlling, and a lover of money, I decided to stay the way I was. Instead of me asking Jesus as my Lord to send my wife the desire to come back to me, I took the matter into my own hands and killed her.

I am the poster child of a domestic violence perpetrator. I had it all twisted up as to what it meant to be a man. I expected my woman to submit, rather I was right or wrong. That means I was prepared to fight if the respect, honor and obedience I expected weren't forthcoming. Not only that, but I needed to feel wanted.

When Janet and I first got together, you could feel the passion between us. Being with her made me feel more wanted than I had ever felt before. She had become my new source of euphoria. "Dang, man, she's really yours!" I'd think whenever I'd look at her and take her all in.

When we first met, both of us had solid careers. She was a manager at Burger King and I was a Team Leader on track to be a manager within a few years. Janet was spiritual and grounded, dedicated to her children, and not looking for love. That made me want her even more.

Eventually we both fell in love but after marriage and our son was born, things changed. I felt the pressures of life gripping me tighter and tighter. Never did I plan for Janet to not be a financial help in the household. But as the mother, the caregiving of our son was mainly her job. So when there was no babysitter, she began to miss work and soon lost her job.

Janet had a God and family over everything mentality. When we were dating, I put my best face forward, and I think she had the impression that we shared those same values. But I wasn't ready to submit to no God, no church or no preacher. Sure I believed in God. I knew about Jesus and church, but I didn't see how any of that made any cash. And in my value system, it was always M.O.E. (Money Over Everything). And if I wasn't getting to the money, then anything within my control was going to bend for me to get it. Janet found that out the hard way.

I had already pleaded that I was a changed man to get back into the house. I wanted to change- to not be without her and Willie Jr. but I wasn't ready to submit to the one thing that could have truly helped me to change. Consequently, I now know that the only true way to change is through a relationship with Jesus Christ.

Once I was back in the house, she discovered my deception. I was still the same money hungry, controlling man. I never thought Janet would EVER leave me for real. Usually, when I got angry and lashed out, I could apologize and just talk to her a little and she'd forgive me. But this time, something had changed. She had made a final decision. I could see it in her eyes when she humiliated me and put me out in front of that delivery driver. I could hear it in her voice when I called, trying to come back home. She wasn't bending the way I wanted her to.

I thought I could juggle having all the control and all her love until she booted me out of the apartment for her and the children's sake. Of course, she was correct. I frightened her. I had become quarrelsome, temperamental, dishonest, and most of all - abusive. I had lost all sense of judgment and rationality. It became about respect with me. "You will respect me!" That was my mantra, even when I wasn't being respectable.

My reaction to being booted out of the apartment was emotionally immature. In my mind, I jumbled her rejection in with all the humiliations from my past. I held her responsible for everything that had gone wrong in my life that day. Oh, if only I had the power to relive that day and make other decisions. However, I am unable to do so. I did everything to erase the recollection of that day the first three years I was incarcerated, but it has remained scorched into my mind. Now that I'm truly mentally ready to take responsibility for my actions, it's a hard pill to swallow that I was the monster that killed my son's mother - my own wife - that fateful day.

After she put me out in front of the delivery guy, I walked around the corner and called her. I tried every tactic I'd ever used to get back in the apartment with her. First anger and threats. Then I pleaded with her to return to me. After I had just threatened her, did I truly believe she'd say yes? I knew I scared her, that I wasn't safe to be around for her or the kids. Deep down, I knew it wasn't her fault, and that she was doing her best. But, in my wrath, I blamed her. And with her making things so final, my mind couldn't stand the notion of her with someone else. Or someone else being there with her and MY SON!

Anger rose in me. I paced and paced. I waited an hour, then I walked back around the corner to the apartment. The delivery guy looking at me like I was some pathetic chump kept flashing in my mind. I just kept thinking, *this disrespect is Janet's fault.* No woman is going to disrespect me like this. I was hot with anger. My eyes were bulging as I searched for an entry way into the apartment. I found an opening in the sliding glass door, got inside and screamed her name. "JANET!" She didn't respond. *More disrespect,* I thought.

When I reached the bedroom doorway, she popped up in the bed, startled. I grabbed her by her beautiful neck, the one I used to kiss at night, and slammed her back down. She attempted to free herself of me, but my strength was no match for the woman who had gently snuggled our son to sleep and caressed my back. I choked and killed her, snuffing out her life. In court, they said it was the blow to her throat that caused her death. They said I tried to kill her oldest son, Adreion, before the men in the neighborhood held me down for the police.

I couldn't recall anything at first. Like when your body falls into shock. I guess the mental fog was some form of self-preservation. Years have passed since the memories surfaced, and I've finally admitted my guilt to myself and to others in group therapy. But I started by blaming everyone else. The truth is, it wasn't my parents' fault. It wasn't Janet's fault or her teenage sons. It was me and my controlling, abusive, money hungry behavior. I felt society had dealt me a poor hand before I finally came to those conclusions.

I am currently incarcerated for the rest of my life. The judge said, I'll never be released. Sometimes I fantasize about getting out of prison, starting a new life, eating decent food again, and preparing a delectable dinner with genuinely fresh ingredients, something I will never be able to accomplish inside. Some nights I allow my dreams to take me wandering in the woods near a stream, where I dip my feet in the cool running water and walk barefoot in lush grass while eating fresh corn and sun-ripened tomatoes on a sunny day. Plants and flowers charm me: living beings that are frail and fleeting yet stunningly lovely. I've grown more conscious of beauty, love, and kindness.

But forgiveness is a notion that I find difficult to grasp. Is it possible for me to even forgive myself for what I did? I don't think Janet's family would ever forgive me, and I wouldn't expect them to. But I owe them the opportunity to tell me how I've damaged their lives; I'm ready and eager to do so. I know that expressing "I am profoundly sorry" won't be enough. Perhaps knowing that I'm doing everything I can to help others avoid our destiny by sharing this part of the story will ease the pain. Or perhaps not.

I'm plagued with feelings of guilt and humiliation. Guilt is the admission of doing something wrong or cruel, but shame is a deep internal feeling of personal unworthiness. Guilt is less terrible than shame; both are unpleasant, but one is about the act, and the other is about the person. I must take responsibility, but not shame. Yes, I am more than my worst act. But there's one thing I still need to do: make amends for what I've done. Except for the atonement paid by Christ on the cross, there is no complete atonement. But I fantasize about utilizing my experience and my story to reach out to other men who are on the verge of doing the same thing I did—before their wrath becomes tragic. I'll have found a vocation for my dying years if I can prevent one man from doing what I did and saving his loved one from Janet's fate.

I'll most likely perish in here. But one option I still have in life is to contribute my voice to one of the most important issues of our time: the empowerment of women to have the ability to speak truth to power. And to help educate men and women about relationships. You rarely hear a voice from the side of the abuser, who has committed the heinous crime yet has the credibility to talk candidly and wisely to other males on the verge of destroying countless lives.

Fellas, you can't beat a woman into respecting you and a woman protecting herself and her kids is not disrespect in the first place. It's her valuing the lives she's brought forth. It's your duty to be their protector on this earth, not the predator they need to hide from.

Ladies, no genuine change comes from anyone by their mere words. Change only comes by accepting Jesus Christ as Lord and then following Him and his ways. If he hasn't done that, then he hasn't changed. I don't care WHAT HE SAYS or how much he begs, pleads, gives you puppy dog faces or tears. No true change can come without Christ!

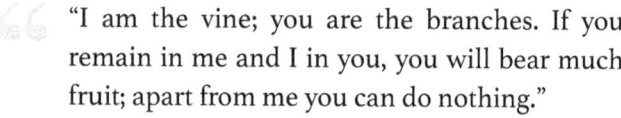 "I am the vine; you are the branches. If you remain in me and I in you, you will bear much fruit; apart from me you can do nothing."

- Jesus
John 15:5 (NIV)

THE END

LEAVE A REVIEW

Like this book?
Reviews are appreciated and welcomed. They can be as long
or as short as you'd like. Even star ratings are wonderful.
Thank you!

JANET SHAW

Broken to Dust is based on a true story. Our father and mother had six children. Together they raised five daughters and one Son. Janet left our family far too soon.

Janet Shaw was a loving and kind daughter, sister, friend and mother. She was a people person and will forever be cherished by her family and her children. She spent many evenings cheering on the University of Alabama as a football fan and enjoying movie nights with her children.

Most of all Janet Shaw loved the Lord and the Bible. The one thing that gives us peace as a family is that she was a follower of Jesus Christ.

We share her story as a warning for other women in domestic violence situations. There were many warning signs in this story based on Janet's life. The National Domestic Violence Hotline has a website at www.thehotline.org where you can get more information to identify abuse, make a plan for safety, and chat with someone for help. You can also call them 24 hours a day at 1-800-799-SAFE or text "Start" to 88788.

Isolation is one of the abuse techniques identified on The National Domestic Violence Hotline website. Please find someone you trust to speak to - a family member, a friend, a church member, or a pastor.

If Janet's story can save another family from a tragic loss then it has been worth reliving to spread her message.

God bless,
From Mary Shaw and Iesha Shaw

ABOUT THE AUTHOR

Iesha Shaw is the proud daughter of William and Mary Shaw. She is an aunt of eleven children. Her nieces and nephews are the reason she chose to become an author and an educator.

She graduated from Walden University College with a Bachelor of Science in Child Development and a Masters Degree in Early Child Development.

You can keep up with Iesha Shaw and the new books that she releases by following her author page on amazon.

amazon.com/author/ieshashaw

ALSO BY IESHA SHAW

My Mother as a Role Model and a LeBron James and Cam Newton Fan: A Devotional for Girls

Teaching Beyond the Chalkboard: A 21-Day Devotional for Teachers

Yes! You Can Do It: Self Love for Black Girls Like Me

The Bear Family Vacation: A Bear Children's Book

The Bear Family Loves You Holiday Series